21 Days of Secrets

21 DAYS OF SECRETS

By

J.J. Jackson

Felony Books, a division of Olive Group, LLC,
P.O. Box 1577, Belton, MO 64012

ISBN-13: 978-1974469284

Felony Books 1st edition September 2017

10 9 8 7 6 5 4 3 2 1

Manufactured in the United States of America

For information regarding special discounts for bulk purchases, please contact Felony Books at felonybooks@gmail.com.

Text **JORDAN** to **77948**

And stay updated on all of Jordan Belcher Presents' *newest releases, free giveaways,* and *special promotions!*

Publisher's Warning:

This title is an *UrbanSnapshot*™, a stand-alone short story charged with suspense, love, and crime.

~Highly Addictive Substance~

Day 1

Shit, I'm running late. My first temp job. Hell it seems like I can't do nothing right these days. If I miss this damn job how I'ma explain that to my P.O.? One more month and I'ma free fuckin woman, Gia thinks to herself as she brushes her teeth. When she's done, she walks into her closet and starts throwing stuff around looking for a pair of shoes to match her suit.

"This clean. Life is so hard for a bitch. Damn, I miss hacking them government computers. Shit was sweet. We made $50,000 a month. I was living on easy street until David got popped. Then his ass decided he wanted to play true confession. And they say women can't hold water. It had'ta been a man that made that lie up. But them was the good old days fo' sho. There you are, my pretty little shoes. I gotta do some'em 'bout this damn closet. 'Cause I know I just straightened this fucka up last week," she says out loud. She takes a look at herself in her mirror, making sure everything looks the part for her new job.

J.J. Jackson

A bitch sho nuff look good. I thank God for Brittany. She gotta be the best booster on this side of the east coast. These Chanel shoes and this three-piece Valentine pinstripe mini skirt suit is setting my sexy ass off. Damn it feels good to be me, Gia adds to her thoughts while slipping her $800 Chanel oversized shades on. She takes one last look.

"Now that's what a bitch talking 'bout. Dang, Gia, you fine," she compliments herself one last time.

Gia has always been a beautiful girl. She's never had any problems getting the man she wants. Well in that case nor has she had problems getting a woman either. Gia's measurement are 48D-23-36. She has long slender legs, a basketball ass, her hair is long, bone straight to be exact. Her skin is flawless, she has light grey eyes with a nice brown complexion as if she has a built-in tan. Her beauty will put any women to shame and she knows it, but it's one thing about Gia—her attitude stinks. If she can't have it then no one can. Gia has always used what God has given her to get whatever it is she wants.

She has no limits.

"Well, it's that time," she says then she leaves her apartment, hops in her convertible all black Mini Cooper, driving off to the sounds of Drake's, "Started From The Bottom."

She weaves in and out of traffic as she drives down Suitland Parkway. When she reaches downtown DC she pulls into the parking garage of her new job assignment located on 19th Street. She gets a ticket then parks her ride. She walks into the building.

"Hold, hold the elevator please!" she yells out, running towards the closing doors.

The young man on the elevator sticks his arm through the door so they won't close. Gia boards the elevator with folders in hand.

"Thank you, sir. I'm running late," she tells him, feeling like she's lost her wind. *A bitch gotta join a gym,* she thinks to herself.

"What floor?" the young man asks.

"Oh, um, shit what floor?" Gia repeats as she fumbles through some papers. She stops at a blue sticky.

"Eight, it's the eighth floor," she says, looking down at the number on the sticky.

"So you're going to Smith Fordham and Burt Accountant firm?" he raps.

"Yes, the largest in the world," she replies, looking him up and down, lowering her shades smiling.

They reach the 3rd floor. Another man boards.

"Hi, Ted," the man on the elevator greets.

"Hi, Bill."

Gia looks at Bill. *Oh my God he is fine as hell. I would serve him breakfast lunch and dinner all at the same time,* Gia is thinking to herself as she feels her kittie start to moisten. Gia drops her folders. Bill and Ted look down. She starts to bend over to pick them up.

"Oh no, let me," Bill says, reaching down to help Gia. Their eyes melt into one.

"What's your name, Gorgeous?" Bill asks her, handing her the folders.

"Giovanni, but everyone calls me Gia for short," she tells him, blushing.

Ding. The elevator sounds off as the doors open.

"Well, this our floor," Bill turns to Ted saying.

"Oh you two work on this floor?" Gia asks.

"Yes we do," the both of them answer in unison.

"Good morning, Mr. Smith," one of the workers greets as Bill enters the office.

"Good morning, Mr. Fordham," another says.

"Good morning, ladies," Bill replies as he looks back at Gia with a slight smirk on his handsome round face.

Gia's heart drops when she realizes she just rode up the elevator with two of the top executives of the largest AA firm in the world. Then she collects her thoughts. *This is gon' be a double blessing,* she's thinking as she walks over to the receptionist desk.

Day 2

"Hi, my name is Gia Shirley. I'm from Master's Temps," she tells the receptionist.

"You're the new temp. Have a seat over there and some-one will be with you," the white young lady orders, pointing to the lobby area full of seats. Then she lowers her head, answering her switchboard as if to say you're dismissed.

"Bitch," Gia mumbles under her breath, turning and walking to the lobby area.

Gia takes a seat. She waits for one hour before an older lady shows up.

"You must be Mrs. Shirley?" the older lady says, hold-ing out her hand for a shake.

"That would be me," Gia responds with a fake smile. She's pissed as hell that she had to wait one whole hour so she doesn't put her hand out for the friendly greet. The lady looks down at her hand. Noticing it's coming up empty, she drops it to her side.

"I'm sorry for the long wait but we had an unexpected board meeting."

"I understand," Gia lies.

"Well, Ms. Shirley, follow me. You'll be working here for 6 months as Mr. Smith's assistant. He's the lead partner of this company. His old assistant went to our office in New York to train for her new position. That makes this position open for hire," she informs Gia.

"Oh, really? That's a good thing for me," Gia tells her with excitement in her voice.

The lady eyeballs Gia, stopping in her tracks.

"Ms. Shirley, you're funny. We don't hire Temps." She tries to get Gia back for not shaking her hand. She's trying to belittle her by looking her up and down. But Gia being Gia thinks fast on her feet.

"Oh no, I didn't mean *I* wanted the job. I meant it's better for me that someone will be taking the position in about six months. Ms. ...?"

The lady finally tells Gia her name. "Oh, it's Mrs. Jones."

"Ok, Mrs. Jones. Because I'll be getting your job," Gia says, then they bust out into laughter.

"You're a very funny lady," Mrs. Jones lets on.

"Only if you knew you're going to be my first victim," Gia says under her breath.

"Ok, Gia, this is your desk right outside Mr. Smith's office. He will tell you what he wants. Now if you have too many mess ups I'll have to call Master Temps and have you replaced. Do I make myself clear?" Mrs. Jones tells her, looking over her glasses.

"Very clear. Tell me something, Mrs. Jones ..."

"Anything."

"Did the temp agency tell you anything about me?"

"No. We just tell them what we want and they send the perfect person for the job every time. We've been dealing with this agency for 25 years so we trust them fully. Is there something we should know about you except that you're a walking label?"

Mrs. Jones strikes again, surveying Gia's gear.

"No. And for the record I'm a good worker who happens to love high fashion," Gia tells her, now scanning her inventory.

Non-dressing bitch, she can't afford my underwear, Gia is thinking.

"Mrs. Jones, what is it that you do here? If you don't mind me asking."

"I'm the head of control. That means—"

"I know what that means. You're the boss," Gia cuts into her sentence.

"Look here, you little—"

"And here comes Mr. Smith," Gia cuts her short again. "Hello again, Mr. Smith," Gia spits with a smile.

Mrs. Jones glances at him. "You two met?"

"Kind of," says Mr. Smith. "I do know I like her, Mrs. Jones. So make sure you treat her as one of the family. Who knows, I may just keep her on board. She seems bright and she's beautiful. We need someone fresh like flowers in this office. Wouldn't you agree?" he asks her, winking at Gia.

"I'll order them flowers right now, Sir," Gia says, picking up the phone feeding into Mr. Smith's sarcasm.

When Bill walks back into his office, "You need anything else?" Gia says with the phone to one ear, a smile on her cute little sneaky face.

"Don't fuck wit' me, young lady," Mrs. Jones lets out, heading down the hall.

"You ain't seen nutten yet. Gia's here, bitch. And I will be the HBIC real soon."

Day 3

"Gia, can you come in my office with your tablet?" Mr. Smith summons her.

"Yes, Sir," Gia says, grabbing her tablet, hurrying to impress her fine ass boss. She is wearing an all-white Ferragamo mini dress with some Tom Ford Croc pumps. She's dressed for sex.

"You rang?" Gia stands in front of his desk and asks.

He looks up. "Uh, um, umm ..." He has to clear his throat, loosen his collar so he can catch his breath.

Why does she have to be so young plus fine all at the same time, he's thinking.

She knows he likes what he's seeing but she plays it off.

"Did you like your coffee?"

"Coffee? Coffee? Oh yes, my coffee. Yes, it was delicious," he says, licking his full lips. Then the office becomes so silent you can hear snow fall.

"Sooo ... what did you want?" Gia asks, taking a seat in one of the chairs positioned in front of his desk. She places the tablet on her lap.

"Want? Oh yeah, what I want ... Oh yeah, Ms. Shirley—"

"Can you please call me Gia?"

"Ok, Gia."

"Thanks," she tells him.

"The company is having its 30th anniversary party next month. This year it's up to me to plan it."

Gia lifts the tablet up off her lap, crosses her legs making sure her skirt raises just enough for him to get a sneak peek. "Good. I love parties. What do you want me to do because I can plan the whole bash. Just give me a budget." She assures him he has the right women for the job.

"Whoo, you just took a load off my shoulders. I have so much to do around here and very little time to do it. Not to mention the fact that I have no idea how to put a small party together, more less talking about one of this magnitude."

"Well that's what you pay me for," she adds.

"The budget is $300,000. And Sherry Thompson that works across the hall ... I'm sure you two have met by now ... she has all the contact information you will need to set everything up. The party is usually held at the Mayflower hotel but you can have it at any nice venue."

"Thanks, Mr. Smith, for putting all your trust in me."

He leans back in his leather captain office chair. "You came in here wearing all these designer suits, looking like you just jumped off the cover of *Elle* magazine. Something is telling me this will be the nicest party we've ever had," he tells her, showing his perfect smile. "Are you married, Gia?"

"I was. But my husband and daughter died in a car accident two years ago," she lies.

"Wow, I'm sorry to hear that," he tells her.

"Don't be. Him and I were over. But my child I will always miss."

She is playing her role. Gia was adopted. She never met her family until she met her twin sister at a party before she got locked up. They ran into one another in the restroom. Gia was coming in and her sister was going out. They bumped into each other. Both of them jumped 'cause they're identical. They could not believe how they found one another. They talked about how they grew up and how they knew they had to have someone out there in the world that they were missing. They exchanged information and kept in contact until Gia got locked up. They lost contact until a few weeks ago when Gia ran into her at the P.O.'s office. Gia doesn't trust her, and for real she really doesn't like her too much but she respects the fact that she's her sister. Her twin did some foul shit to her in the past that she wasn't feeling

21

but she felt like she needed to forgive her; after all, she is her blood—the only blood she knows.

"Is there anything else I can do for you?" she asks him.

"No, that will be all."

Gia raises up, struts out his office bouncing her basket balls a little harder than normal, hoping he's looking.

I know he's watching, she's thinking as she starts to close his door behind her. Before she could get it closed:

"It may be one more thing," he says, star gazing. "Can you stay a little late tonight? I may need your help with these weekly stats."

"That wouldn't be a problem. But tonight I'm taking my father to the game to see the Wizards. How about tomorrow?" She tells another lie.

"That'a be great. Tomorrow it is. And Gia that is so nice of you to take your father to the game? How old is he?"

"Seventy. He can't walk." Another lie she tells before exiting his office.

"Damn, I hated to turn his fine ass down. He looks so freakin' good. I mean he could be my man. He reminds me of my ex. That black muthafucka could lay down the law in bed. And that Ted, his partner, looks like a George Clooney. I guess I'll have to see who has the biggest cut. Only time will tell," she whispers to herself, walking across the hall to Sherry's office.

"Hey, Sherry, I'm—"

"I know who you are. And as far as I'm concerned you're just the Temp—and it's *Ms. Thompson* to you. Here is the rolodex. And please don't ask me for help. I got enough shit to do around here. For the record, I'm not your friend. I don't wanna be. So don't ask me to eat wit' you or go out wit' you. I don't hang wit' the help," Sherry tells her in one breath.

"That's fine wit' me, secretary!" Gia snaps back.

"What did you say?"

"You heard me. Did I st-st-studda, bitch," Gia whispers, gritting on her with disgust written all over her face.

"Fuck with me, little girl, I'll have your job," Sherry whispers back through clenched teeth.

"Hell, you can have it since I know it pays more than yours," Gia strikes back as she walks out her office, back across the hall to her outer office space. "I see I'ma have'ta show and prove around here. These bitches are so jelly. But that's ok 'cause I'll be at the top of the food chain before McDonalds comes up wit' a new burger."

Day 4

"It's Wednesday, getting over the hump day. A bitch like me is sick of this 9 to 5 shit already." Gia sits in her living room talking out loud to no one but herself, as always. She picks up a paper that lays on her coffee table.

Gia has been working all day on this event. She's called venues and they are all booked; all but one—the JW Marriott. So she takes the date they have quickly. Then she calls Janet Flowers, the best in the DC area. The event planner at the hotel told her they would take care of the food. She faxed Gia over a copy of the menu. Gia picked shrimp, jumbo crab cakes, goat cheese, string beans, chicken breast, ham, champagne, a host of sweets coffee and Teas as well. She took the money to the event planner, then she called her booster Brittany to hook her up with something hot for the party. She has to go today to taste test some of the food and that she is looking forward to. She picks up her phone to call her friend. He answers.

"Hi, boo," he calls her.

"Hey, Jason. You coming through tonight?"

"I gotta pick up my daughter."

"Jason, my ass is so horny. I know you can come over for an hour or so. Can't your daughter wait?" she asks her fuck partner.

"No, Gia. And that's so selfish of you to even ask. Nobody comes before her."

"You always do this shit. I need your ass bad. Hell, it's been five days," Gia squeals.

"It hasn't. It's only been two. Besides, didn't you tell me I can't be beaten that pussy up 'cause you's a worka girl now?" he reminds her with his Jamaican accent.

"Whateva!" she shouts, then hangs up in his ear. "Men—you can't live wit'em, can't live without'em!" she screams out loud.

Rushing, she goes to her dresser drawer, she pulls out her silver bullet, lays on her bed, pulls her shorts to the side, spreads her legs apart, turns the bullet on, presses it to her hard clit to relive the feeling she's having. She moans as the vibration of the bullet caresses her kitty; it goes round and round.

"Sissss ... yes oh yes," she moans as her mind goes to ecstasy. When she's about to cum she hears the sounds of her cell ringing. She jumps up and answers it.

"Hello?"

"Gia, this is Mrs. Jones. I was just checking to see if you did all that needs to be done for the party."

Oh how I hate this bitch, Gia is thinking.

"Yes, everything is done. Mrs. Jones, it would be nice if you could wait until work hours to call me about small stuff. I do have a life, you know," Gia converses.

"Well you do work for me. I do need to know things so I'll call you when I need you," she fires back.

"Correction: I work for the company and you don't sign my check. The Temp agency does."

Click. Gia hangs up on in her ear.

"That bitch interrupting my sex session for some bullshit. But it's ok, I got a surprise that will make that old hoe pop out her eyes."

Day 5

It's Thursday morning. Gia wakes up to the birds humming and the sun shining through her large bay window.

"What time is it?" She yawns, looking over at the clock on her nightstand.

"Oh shit, I'm late! It's fuckin' eight. I'm not gon make it by 8:30, it's no way. Ok, Gia, think fast. Shit, let me call Bill ... fuck, he probably not in yet! I got it—I'll call the lady at the JW and tell her I'm going to drop in this morning."

Gia picks up her house phone, dials the event planner at the JW Marriott.

"JW Marriott, how my I direct your call?" the operator addresses.

"Yes, my name is Ms. Shirley. I'm planning a party that will take place there next month. I would like to come through this morning to check out the Ballroom."

"Ms. Shirley, let me direct your call to Mrs. Bryant. Please hold."

Gia stands by listening to the sounds of Kenny G's "Songbird."

Thirty seconds later, "Ms. Shirley, how are you today?" the chipper voice of Mrs. Bryant comes on the line.

"I'm fine, thank you."

"I hear you would like to come through this morning to check out the Ballrooms?"

"Yes, I would. If that's possible?" Gia's at her mercy.

"Ms. Shirley, that will be fine by me. Do you know what time you would like to come through?"

"About nine this morning, if that's ok with you."

"I'll clear my calendar. See you at nine this morning," Mrs. Bryant returns.

"Thanks. See you then." Gia is relived.

Now I have my excuse, Gia ponders as she gets ready.

After she's dressed, she dials her job.

"Smith, Fordham & Burt," the receptionist answers.

"This is Gia Shirley. I won't be in until 12 noon or so—"

"What's your excuse?" the receptionist quickly spits.

"None for you. But you can transfer me to Mr. Smith's voicemail, thanks," Gia politely comments.

Click.

"Oh hell no she didn't. That bitch!" Gia yells.

Then she dials the office again. After the first ring the receptionist answers.

"Smith—"

Gia cuts her off right away. "I'ma cut your tongue out your mouth and watch you die a slow death. You can count on it!" Gia whispers, then hangs up the phone laughing. "Mrs. Jones was gon' be my fist Victim but I've changed my mind. It's gon' be that ratchet ass white bitch," she murmurs while putting on her makeup, continuing to laugh.

She meets with Mrs. Bryant then she goes to work. She walks into the office straight to the receptionist desk.

"Excuse me, I think you hung up on me," Gia communicates real nice like.

"You think? Well, you not paid to think," the receptionist informs her, rolling her eyes, throwing her long blond hair back.

"I would like to call a truce. I brought you some cupcakes from Sweet Tooth's Bakery. They make the best in town," Gia says with a smile across her face.

"Well, you can put them over there. I don't want'em," she verbalizes wit' an attitude.

"Aw c'mon, they're delicious." Gia takes a bit out of one of them.

"Well maybe one of them won't hurt. I'm trying to watch my girlish figure, you know."

Gia hands her the cupcake with the red frosting on it. "Here, take this one. Red is my favorite color." Gia should have grew up in Hollywood, California, 'cause she's a great actress.

"*Ummm* ... this is good, Gia," she talks with her mouth full.

"See, I told you." Gia leaves the other cupcakes on her desk. And true to Gia's thinking, she eats one more of them. And within ten minutes ...

"Uh ... uh ... *whoo* ... my stomach didn't like them cupcakes as much as my mouth did." The receptionist holds her stomach, calling over the intercom to Sherry. "Can you come and take over for me. I gotta go to the restroom, Sherry."

"Sure, I'll be right there."

When Sherry appears, the receptionist jumps up holding her stomach. She rushes to the restroom. She barely gets her skirt up and her underwear off before her turtles start to come out.

She sits on the toilet.

Bluuuu-bluuss!

She starts shitting right away. She looks up and sees Gia standing right in front of her with the stall door open.

"What you doing in here? Get out, I'm shittin'." Her stomach is cramping too much for her to even fuss.

"I just wanted to make sure you was ok," Gia tells her.

"Well I'm *ohh—Ahhhh.*"

Gia starts choking her around her neck. "You hung up on me this morning. I told you I was gon' cut your tongue out." Gia takes the tongs that's in her other hand and pinches her tongue with them. "Now hold still. I'ma make this quick and painful." Gia lets her neck go and brings her hand down with the razor blade in it, then she stops short of the tip of the receptionist's tongue. She bursts out laughing, then she lets go. The receptionist feels so relieved. She really thought Gia was going to make her tongue-less.

"That shit ain't funny, you black bitch. You scared the hell outta me! You stupid bitch!" she's yelling and pushing Gia's hands away from her. Gia glares down at her.

"I know I shouldn't have scared you like that. I'm sorry but I would never cut your tongue out. But I will do this."

Gia pulls a needle out of her pocket. Quickly she jams it in the side of her neck, pushing the poison into the receptionist's veins. She instantly keels over and dies a quick death. Gia stands over her corpse.

"I really, really wanted to keep my word and watch you die a slow death. Momma said a woman is nothing without her word. But in this case cutting your fuckin' tongue out would've been too messy. Too much blood for this time of day. You's a lucky bitch."

Gia quickly moves out the stall, washes her hands, opens the restroom door. She checks her surroundings, then makes her get away. She sashays to her desk like nothing ever happened.

Day 6

"I can't believe what happened to Lisa the receptionist," one of the ladies whispers to another co-worker in the office.

"Me either. I mean how did she die anyway?" another lady says.

"They don't know," Sherry chimes. "All I know is she called me to take over the switchboard while she went to the restroom. The damn board was so busy, time got past me. When I did look down at my watch I noticed thirty minutes had passed so I ask Danna—you know her, the red hair older lady that cleans the office?"

"Yeah," one of the ladies cuts in.

"Well, she went to see if Lisa was still in the restroom. Then all of a sudden I see Danna running towards me screaming, 'She's dead, she's dead! Her eyes still open! She's dead!' She looked like she had just saw a ghost. She grabbed her stuff and told me she quit. I got up and walked to the restroom myself. After seeing what I saw I ran to Mr.

Smith's office to tell him, then that bitch Gia was like what's wrong what happened. I told her and she called the police," Sherry explains. They all gasp.

"You poor girl. You musta been shocked?" Mrs. Jones hugs her.

"Shocked is not the word, Mrs. Jones."

"Maybe she had something and she didn't tell nobody," one of the women who's eavesdropping says.

"Who knows with these young girls," Mrs. Martha, the office manager, chimes in.

"Oh well, life goes on. I have to get back to work," Sherry spits. As she turns to walk away, Gia rolls up. They exchange words.

"Who is that pretty young lady?" one of the older ladies needs to know.

"She's the new temp. She's working for Mr. Smith," Mrs. Jones returns.

"Mr. Smith is sure to fuck that one," Martha remarks.

"Martha, hush your mouth. He's a married and a very respectful man, I have you know," Mrs. Jones tells her, disgusted with what she just said in front of the other employees.

"He's not too respectful. Let's not forget he got caught with Susan in the restroom as a matter of fact. The same one they just found that girl in ... dead as a door knob."

"Remind me never to use that damn restroom again, eva in life," Janise, the head of finances, exclaims.

"But Martha you don't even know if that's true. That could've been a rumor on this job," Mrs. Jones assures them all.

"Well, he's a man with a dick that still gets hard. I don't put nothing past none of 'em. I do know that girl is bewitching and he's a sucker for a young pretty face so I think all y'all need to watch out for your jobs. Look at Susan; she was transferred to New York, and now she's our boss. So what does that tell you?"

"On that note, I'm going downstairs back to my office where life is simple," Janise mutters and bows out this time.

"That sounds good to me. As a matter of speaking, we all need to get back to work. Back to work, ladies." Martha claps her hands and orders.

***

Gia enters Bill's office.

"Mr. Smith, do you have a minute?"

"Yes, do come in. Take a seat." He's having a conversation with his partner Ted. "What is it, Gia?" Bill gives her his undivided attention.

"I just wanted to tell you I can stay late tonight if you need anything. I'm done with the project you gave me."

"Gia, you're such a good worker. I'm not going to need you tonight. Janise is going to help me in the boardroom but maybe tomorrow night," Bill informs her.

"Bill, I may need her tomorrow. I'm having trouble with the Mason account. Maybe she can do my spreadsheets for me while I go over the numbers."

"Well, Gia, would you like to help Ted?"

"Sure, why not." Her voice is real chipper. She's still standing in his office.

"Will that be all?" Bill is short with her.

"Yes, Sir," she tells him, walking out of his off.

I'm going to fuck his brains out. And Bill you're going to be next. They just don't know who they hired.

Day 7

It's a new day. The sun is shining, the weather crisp. Gia is feeling well rested as she makes a beeline to her office. She places her fresh flowers in the empty vase that sets on her desk, then she does her everyday duties—pours Mr. Smith a hot black cup of decaf coffee, sets it on his desk ever so gently, turns his computer on, pulling the day's rates up.

She goes back to her office, turns on her computer, pulling up the work for today. Gia's really loving her job but she wants the top position. She does her job well as she tiptoes around all the haters, but this is something she's been accustomed to all her life. This is nothing she can't handle. Plus she's not a people person anyway.

She makes her last phone call, then puts in her last report.

"Gia, you're doing a good job. I wish you were here a long time ago. My workload is so much lighter now that we've found you," Bill compliments her.

"Thank you, Sir—"

"Gia, please call me Bill. You're my assistant, the closest person to me right now so do call me Bill," he retorts.

"Whatever you say, Bill." She smiles.

"I'm leaving for tonight but remember you told Ted you would help him with those spreadsheets. If it's anything you don't understand you let him know. I'm sure Harvard University prepared you for anything he shoots your way."

I almost forgot I put Harvard on my app.

"Yes they did. I can' wait to see what he has in store for me tonight."

Even though she lied to the Temp company about where she got her credentials, when she was in the military they put her through school. She earned her Accounting degree then she went to Howard University and earned her Masters. Gia knows more than most of the workers in the department.

Leaning over he whispers in her ear, "You'll do great. But Gia don't show him out. Let him feel like he knows a little something," Gia hears him but then again she doesn't 'cause she's too busy enjoying the smell of his cologne.

"I won't, I promise."

Everyone has left, even the cleaning crew. Gia goes to the restroom, giving herself a makeover. She returns to her desk, flicks her light switch to off, then paces herself towards Ted's office.

Knock, knock. She knocks on his door that's ajar.

"Hi, Gia, come in," he says, sitting behind his desk scanning his computer.

The lovely Gia struts her way across his office dressed in a Pink Prabal Gurung dress priced at $3,200. She's also sporting some Jil Sander shoes, priced at $900. Gia looks the part even though she didn't pay full price but who knows that but her and her booster. She takes a seat in the chair adjacent from his desk.

"What is it you would like for me to do?" she asks, licking the top of her lips just so, making sure she doesn't mess up her natural color Lip Gloss by Nass.

"If you come over here I can show you these damn spreadsheets. They're a piece of work."

"Sure." She gets up, making her way over to join Ted. She bends over him so she can get a close look at what it is he wants her to do. He starts explaining what he needs done.

"These are the spreadsheets. You have to make sure the number on this side of the spreadsheet matches this side. You also have to be careful 'cause some of the numbers look alike but they're not."

"If they don't match, then what?" she asks.

"Then you'll have to go to that computer over there." He points at a table that's in front of his window. "That computer is the Error in the Hole computer. You input the bad number and it gives you a new number to add to this sheet. After you put the new number on this sheet it will be added to what we call the Blackout list."

"Oh, is that the Department downstairs?" she quizzes.

He looks up at her. Their eyes bounce off one another's.

"Gia, I'm married." He feels he has to tell her. She acts like she doesn't hear a word he's saying by cutting him off. She places her lips over his, making sure she covers his whole mouth.

"Oh my God," Ted mumbles, feeling his nature raising.

Gia caresses his hard penis with the tips of her fingers.

"Yes, that's what I'm talking 'bout. Nice and hard. Now where were we?" She's running her fingers through his jet black silky hair.

Ted just sits there speechless. Gia moves the papers that's in front of him to the side of his desk, then hops up on it, leaning back on her elbows. She opens her legs so Ted can see the pinkness of her pussy. Ted becomes broken as he sees her freshly manicured pussy hairs. She has them cut into one straight line. She places her right hand on her right tender young breast then she licks and sucks the hard nipple that's before her. Ted stands and pulls his pants all the way off, exposing his tighty whities. He's positioned in front of her, massaging his little six-inch pink dick through his undies. Gia scoots to the edge of the desk, eager to get this over with.

"Put it in my wet pussy, big daddy." She feeds his ego. Ted pulls his whites off and does just that. He slides his little man inside her wetness, taking in the warmth of her body. He exhales. He starts to move slowly, rolling his eyes to the back of his head, rocking back and forth on his heels.

"Ohh this feels so good," he repeats over and over until his mouth feels like cotton.

I wish this muthafucka would hurry up and cum already wit' this little ass dick, are her thoughts.

Gia relaxes her head backward, closes her eyes thinking if she just relaxes and thinks of a big black dick maybe she can get some enjoyment out of it.

"Fuck me ... fuck me, daddy!" she moans.

Ted starts to pick up the pace a bit.

"Yes, baby. Make love to this pussy. Give it to me, baby ... shit, fuck this pussy," she acts out as Ted thrusts in and out.

"Oh, Gia, Gia, Gia," Ted whispers.

Ted starts pumping faster, rocking the desk. Papers are falling on the floor. Ted grabs Gia around her neck, squeezing tightly. Now Gia is waking up as her body starts to tingle.

"Uhmmmm ... mmmm shit! Ted, get this pussy. That's what a bitch talking 'bout," she mummers through breaths. He grabs her neck harder as he feels himself getting ready to release his fluids inside her.

"Gia, I'm cumming, Teddy's cumming!" he yells. "Shit oh shit!" Ted continues to yell as he shoots his nut all in her hot pussy.

But Gia continues to grind on his soft dick, causing it to get back up. She thrusts and grinds on his dick for about five minutes.

"Gia, Gia, oh my Gia, I'm cumming again!" Ted groans, filling the walls of her wetness with his cum, one more time.

"Me too ... daddy more-bucks, me too." She's lying. "Oh, Ted, taste my cum," she demands. Ted pulls his dick out, kneels, sucking all Gia's cum out her pussy. Then he stands up and jerks his dick as he raises to his tiptoes. Gia jumps off his desk, bends over and sucks his dick.

"Awwwwh shit, Gia. Oh my goodness here I cum." Ted squirts nut in Gia's mouth. She gargles then she stands and places her mouth over his, allowing his nut to flow from her mouth to his. She hawk eyes him.

"Now *you* swallow," she tells him with a devilish smirk on her face.

Ted is good at following orders.

Day 8

Two down. Ted is so high off my pussy he doesn't know what to do. We fucked until ten last night, then he called my cell at 12 midnight, as if he could come over. His ass is gone already. "Damn, kitty, you really got his ass purring, didn't you?" she says, looking down at her pussy, nodding her head like what a shame

Ring.

Who in the hell is it at this time of the morning?

"Hello?" she answers.

"Hi, may I speak with Ms. Shirley?"

"This is she."

"Hi, Ms. Shirley, this is Mrs. Bryant from the JW."

"Hi, how may I help you this early in the morning?" Gia is being funny.

"I was calling to ask you if you would like two types of toss greens, because you ordered the one that has nuts in the ingredients," she informs her.

"I know, I picked the menu." Gia's baffled.

"Well when I checked the roster I found that you all have an employee that is allergic to nuts."

"Oh really, who might that person be?"

"Let me see here ... here it is ... A Mrs. Jones, Mrs. Allen Jones," the events planner tells her.

"That's too bad. We'll have to change that then. Go ahead and add the one without nuts as well. Thank you for the information 'cause that could've been fatal." Gia acts concern.

"It's nothing. That's my job, but you're welcome."

"Is there anything else I need to know, Mrs. Bryant?"

"No, I think that covers it, but if I run across anything else I'll call you for sure," she tells Gia all chipper like. Then they end their call.

"She's allergic to nuts, huh?" Gia says to herself as she goes back to eating her breakfast.

After eating, she takes a shower then gets dressed. She hops in her car, headed to Dan's Bakery. Pulling up 15 minutes later she parks her car, walks inside.

"Hey, Dan, long time no see," she greets. He's standing behind his backer counter with a white apron on and a long white chef hat on his head.

"Why hello, Vicky. It's been too long." Vicky is the name Gia gave him when she fucked his brains out two months ago. "Damn, you looking rich and fine as ever."

"Thanks."

"What brings you through?"

"Dan, I need a cake baked with peanuts in it crushed up real fine. I don't want to be able to see them. My client is funny about crunching on nuts. I don't want her to be able to taste them either. I'm trying to turn her on to some new things but I want it to be pleasing to her at the same time. You know what I mean?"

"Boy, do I," Dan says with lust in his eyes. "When would you like this cake?"

"Lunch time. Can you make that happen?" she asks, pulling up her skirt exposing her Mohawk pussy.

"Yeah, anything for an old friend." He smiles.

***

Thirty minutes has passed. Gia walks out the bakery feeling refreshed.

That Dan sho can eat some kat. I came three times. Damn, if he wasn't so broke I would marry his ass then kill'em for the insurance policy but his policy is only worth $100,000. That's why I stopped fucking his ass in the first place, but this kill will be worth all the head he just gave me and more, she's thinking as she starts up her car.

She calls the office to let her boss know she's going to be in at one because she has to stop past the JW to handle some of the arrangements. He tells her he'll see her when she gets in to take her time.

Gia does some window shopping, grabs some lunch then heads back to Dan's bakery, picking up the cake. She heads for work—of course after Dan licks her kitty one more time.

She reaches her office, sways in, greets the new receptionist then she stops by Mrs. Allen Jones' office. Gia sticks her head in the door.

"Good, no one's here." She places the cake on the desk, grabs a sticky paper, writes a note. *Thanks for all your hard work, you know who.* She also draws a happy face on it. She lays it on the cake box then she makes her exit unnoticed.

Day 9

"Martha, come here, come here," Janise calls her in a low voice from her office.

"What, girl why we whispering?" Martha whispers.

"Shut the door," she tells her friend. Martha does just that.

"Did you hear?"

"Here what?"

"It's Allen. She's in a coma."

"A what!" Martha's dumbfounded.

"One of the girls from the mailroom found her unconscious on her office floor yesterday. The police been in here all morning. You just missed them."

"On the floor unconscious?! What happened, how did she fall out?" Martha huffs.

"I don't know but I'ma get to the bottom of it."

"What do you mean to the bottom of it? You think somebody did something to'a?" Martha adds all big-eyed.

"No, they say she's allergic to peanuts and that's what the doctors found in her system."

"Peanuts? Why on earth would she eat'em if she's allergic to'em?" Martha's lost.

"They say it was an unfinished cake on her desk with crumbs around her mouth. Rick from the Blackout accounts said she offered him some. He told the police he didn't taste no peanuts in the cake. He added that the damn cake was good. When they asked him did he know where she got the cake from he told them he didn't know. Then they questioned Bill and Ted. They said they didn't know how she got the cake. Then they asked all of us if we gave it to her 'cause it was a note on her desk somebody wrote her, as if someone from here gave her the cake as a reward for her good work. They are asking that we all do a handwriting analysis. That bitch Sherry told them you may have given her the cake since you two are close. Girl, it's getting' hot in *herre*!"

"Me ...? I didn't get her no cake. Why didn't anyone call me last night or this morning to tell me about this shit?!"

"I'on know but this I do know: shit getting' ready to hit the fan," Janise murmurs.

"Do you think somebody's tryna kill'a?" Martha is still stuck on stupid.

"Like I said ... I don't know, but this I do know: first it was that poor receptionist, now it's Allen. If you put two and two together all this shit didn't start until that Temp girl came." Janise is being messy.

"My God! You think she's a killer? But why ... why would she kill a receptionist? It's nothing to gain by killing her. She's already making more, and the girl wears expensive clothes. Hell I can't even afford the stuff she wears." Martha lets it be known.

"I hear she's dating one of them gangsta guys ... you know, a drug dealer." Janise is making stuff up now.

Martha gasps, covering her mouth with her hand. But little do they both know Gia is standing outside the door.

"Knock ... knock," Gia voices as she opens Janise's door. She enters, smiling.

"Hi, how are you?" Martha inquires, clearing her throat.

"I hope I didn't interrupt anything important," Gia says.

"Oh no. How can we help you, Ms. Gia?" Janise parts her lips, glancing over at Martha to let her know that is Gia, even though she knows already.

"In light of everything that's happened around here, I bought this card and some flowers for Allen's family. Would you two like to sign it?" Gia remarks, holding out the card and a black pen towards them.

"Why yes, I think that's nice of you, Gia, being as though you just got here," Janise huffs, not buying the nice girl act one bit.

They both sign the card.

"Thanks." Gia begins to withdraw herself from the office, then she looks back. "Oh yeah, Mrs. Martha, I was wondering if you could help me with some work Mr. Smith gave me. Some of the numbers I'm not too sure of. Since you've been here for 20 years. Well, I—"

"Say no more, honey. Of course Martha will help you. Won't you, Martha," Janise interrupts Gia while glancing over at her longtime friend reading her facial expression.

"What time?" Gia probes Martha.

"How about tonight around six. You can meet me at Gladys Knight's Chicken & Waffles. Do you know where it is?" Martha quizzes.

"No, but I have a friend that eats there all the time. I'll find it."

"That's good. Don't forget to bring your files." Janise is being messy again.

"I won't. Thank you so much," Gia tells the two of them as she scampers from the office. "They think they're going to stop shit. I got some'em for they asses," Gia mumbles under her breath as she makes her way back to her desk. She hits her intercom button.

"Bill, I have to make a run. May I have the rest of the day off?"

"Sure, but can you send flowers to my wife first. It's our anniversary, I almost forgot."

49

"Congratulations," she tells him.

"Thanks."

"I'll have to give you a gift."

"That will be all, Gia," he rudely says.

"Did I offend you?"

"No, you could never do that."

"Ok, have a good night," she chirps.

"I will, thanks."

He's playing hard to get but he'll break. They all do, she thinks while placing the call to the florist.

Day 10

It's 7:00 a.m. Gia's sitting in her living room watching TV.

I'm so happy we're off this weekend. That damn job works you like'a slave, she thinks, placing her cup of tea between her pouched lips.

"Good morning and welcome to ABC News Center. We bring you troubling news this morning as Rhonda Chung reports from Suitland, Maryland. Hi Ronda."

"Hi Mack, I'm reporting live in front of Don's Bakery, where Maryland police are investigating Don the baker's death. He was found this morning with a gunshot wound to the head. No one seemed to hear anything. It's a sad day in this quiet part of town. Don's Bakery was a trademark here in Suitland Shopping Center. Other business owners are shocked, saying Don was a good man and he did many things for the neighborhood children. This community is very upset about this sad and costly tragedy. Police are asking if anyone has seen or heard anything. Please contact the local authorities. Mack, back to you."

"I can't believe this. They found him already," Gia sits back in her chair whispering to herself. "My pussy sho gon' miss his tongue but he had to go 'cause I know his ass would've talked. When Bill told me the police was going to Dan's bakery to find out who bought that type of cake I know I had to kill'em. Why did he have to order platters with his company name and logo? They would've never knew where the cake came from. He would be still alive to this day. Now I gotta get Mrs. Martha's ass. She canceled our dinner date until tomorrow but she's as good as gone. She just don't know it yet."

Tap tap tap. Someone is at Gia's front door.

"Who's there?"

"It's me."

"Here I come!" Gia yells as she rises and opens her door. "Hi, baby, do come in," she yaps in a sexy way.

"Hi, yourself," Ted welcomes, hugging Gia around her tiny waist.

"Um ... you want some morning pussy, don't you?"

"You know daddy do." He cheeses with pleasure.

"I was thinking we do something new," she lets out.

"And what might that be?"

"Are you down for what eva?" She has a smirk on her face.

"You know it."

Only if he knew what he just signed up for.

They go to her room.

"Ok, take off all your clothes. Put on this blindfold," she demands.

"Oh, you're getting kinky on me." Ted does what's asked of him.

She pulls out white handcuffs. "Lay on the bed, face down," she directs.

She handcuffs both wrists and ankles to the bedpost.

"Gia, what are you going to do with me?" He's getting curious.

"Don't worry, daddy. We're gon' have ourselves a ball." She giggles. "Now you wait right there."

Gia returns in about one minute flat. Ted is lying on the bed, ass up.

"I'm back, baby. Now tell me how this feels."

In seconds Ted feels a wet long tongue licking his ass-hole over and over really fast. Ted's ass wiggles.

"Aw ... uh oh ... yes, Gia, right there that feels so good," Ted moans.

"Lift your butt in the air," she directs.

He does it. With her hand full of warm gel she reaches around him and starts jerking his small dick.

"Yes, baby, yes. Gia baby, you're going to make Big Teddy milky."

He must mean little teddy, she thinks as she continues to please him. He's not prepared for what comes next.

"Awwww, Aweee *nooooo!*" Ted yells as his ass starts to raise up and down from the unwanted actions she's delivering.

"Oh, Ted, stop grumblin'. Relax. Relax. This is the best part."

"Awww! Gia, that shit hurts. What is it?"

"I know it hurts. Baby but you said you wanted to play. It'll feel better soon," Gia promises as she continues to ram the nine-inch rubber dildo in and out his ass.

After a while Ted starts catching the rhythm of the handheld dildo. Ted starts to relax as the hole of his ass opens wider with every stroke. His dick starts to jump as it grows hard as a rock.

"Oh shit, Gia, shit!" is all he can say as nut flows from his penis onto her white sheet. Tears flow down his checks from the shame of enjoying the unnatural sexual escapade that's unfolding right before him.

"You like that, baby?" Gia asks. As much as he hated to admit it, he does. "You want more?"

"I do. I do. Please, I do." Ted becomes shameless.

"Not now. We're going to do something different."

"What eva you say."

Gia pulls the dick out Ted's ass. "I'll be right back, daddy. Now don't you move," she says in a childlike voice.

Then she grabs a glass case off the table. She returns to his bedside.

"I'm back. Now where were we?" she utters.

Gia spreads Ted's ass cheeks apart, lubing his asshole really good with warm gel.

"Yes, Gia. Now that feels really good. It's nothing like a butt massage. Gia, please your daddy," he mummers.

"I am. I am." She pulls out a baby gerbil, puts it at the tip of Ted's asshole.

"You ready?" She giggles.

Yes, yes, he eagerly nods.

"Here we go." She lets the gerbil go. It enters his ass head first.

"OOOOOOOh! Noooooo! No what's that I don't like it Gia what is it?!"

Ignoring his cries, she picks up the next one and lets it loose. Ted is howling and squealing.

"AHHHH! STOP MY GOD WHAT IS IT?!" Ted is squirming but he can't get loose.

"Relax, Ted, and enjoy it. My boyfriends love this game. It's called the mousetrap. Let's see how many you can hold."

"GIA, PLEASE! I don't like this one! Go get the dildo please I will let you fuck me again with it, but not this! What is that?! I can feel it moving in my stomach, Gia! I don't want it in me, PLEASE! I don't like this!" he yells.

Warm streams of salt water flow down his face.

"Ted, they're just little baby gerbils. I can go get their mother and father," she teases.

"Ger—WHAT DID YOU SAY A GERBIL?! Gia ... Gia please don't ... do this to me, STOP! It's not fun anymore!"

"Ok you little baby boy." Gia places cheese at the tip of his ass, summoning the gerbils. She places them back in the glass case as they come out one by one. She removes his blindfold.

"Now before I uncuff you, you have to lick me dry." Gia loves herself some good head.

"Ok ... ok," he says, embarrassed and relieved all at the same time.

After he pleasures her, she gets up.

"We done, right? I can go?" he asks, hoping the answer would be yes.

"Yeah, you party pooper. After I go to the bathroom I'll uncuff your baby ass." She's irritated so she pouts all the way to the next room, pulling out the recorded tape.

"I got you now ... you son of a bitch. I'll be head of control by next week. Men—they're so dumb," Gia chats to herself, putting the tape in her hiding spot.

Day 11

Gia stops by the coffee shop to pick up some donuts. She strolls up to the counter.

"Good morning. I need two dozen donuts, please."

"What kind would you like?" the cashier asks.

"The same as I always get."

"I'm new. I just started toda—"

"I'll take care of her," one of the other workers says. She starts fixing Gia's usual.

"Gail Rice!" one of the customers yells out, making her way to face Gia. "Gail!" she howls again, tapping Gia on her shoulder.

Gia swings around, searching the lady over like she's crazy. "Excuse me?" Gia utters.

"You don't remember me? It's Pattie from Wilson and Johnson. You know Pattie girl your old manager. I'm sorry about how Peter did you. He shouldn't have fired you like that. It's just that so much was going on and all the accusations against you and him. His wife—"

"You must be mistaken. I'm not Gail nor do I know any one named Gail. Most of all I don't know a Pattie or a Peter." Gia acts baffled.

"I'm sorry. You look just like her, beautiful as ever. But you're right because Gail got locked up for hacking Wilson and Johnson's computers. She tapped into the government computers as well, through one of our biggest client's accounts. That's when Peter started letting people go. The company became bankrupt," she yaps in one breath.

"I'm sorry to hear that. Maybe one day you will find the lady you seem eager to tell all this unwanted information," Gia delivers with a slight smile across her face.

"That will be $12.50," the cashier chimes in after rubbernecking.

Gia hurries and pays her bill then flees the shop.

"What in the hell is Pattie doing in DC? Shit, that was when I was in Texas. This world is too gotdamn small. You can't even relocate to rid yourself of cockroaches. I'm thinking should I double back and exterminate her ass?" Gia utters to herself, opening her car door.

***

Forty minutes later Gia is pulling into the garage of her job. She parks her car on the lower deck, pulls a silver vibrating bullet out her purse. She glances out her car window, taking stock of her surroundings.

"Boy do I need you. I'm so mad and horny I need to relieve all this tension." She's talking to herself again.

Lifting her skirt up, pulling her thong to the side, she places the bullet on her clit just so and flips the switch. After about 1 minute in heaven,

"Noooo ... oh HELL NO! My fuckin' batteries ran out. *Shit.* I need some fuckin' batteries." She's going crazy looking through her glove compartment, on the floor, in the ash tray, she's digging in her purse.

All of a sudden—*tap, tap.*

She jumps with the bullet in hand. She starts her car up to let down the window.

"What is it, Sherry?" she snaps with irritation.

Sherry grins, holding up a pack of batteries. "You need these. Ha ha ha," she starts laughing her ass off.

"Fuck you, bitch," Gia shouts, letting her window back up.

I'm gon kill'a. If it's the last thing I do, she tells herself.

Gia lets herself out of her car, grabbing hold of the donuts. She heads into the office. Everyone is looking at her funny but Gia is being Gia, letting on like she notices nothing at all.

She peeps in his office. "Good morning, Bill," she greets.

"Good morning, Gia. Can you make sure everyone is in the boardroom by 10:00 this morning?"

"Will do, Sir," she said to Bill.

"Thanks. Put the receipt on Sherry's desk for the donuts so we can reimburse you," he tells her, never looking up.

"No problem." She carries out his orders.

It's 10:00 a.m. Everyone is gathered in the huge board-room that's stationed on the 4th floor of the building. Ted makes his way in, then Bill, who takes a seat in between Martha and Janise at the table.

"Ok, everyone. First of all I'm proud to say that all the department heads have been really doing a great job in spite of what has transpired over the last couple of weeks. I must inform you all that Allen Jones is doing better. She is still in and out of her coma but the doctors thinks she will come around."

They all clap, including Gia.

"However, a company of this magnitude must go on in spite of. Now I don't mean to sound insensitive but we must hire a new person for control. Mrs. Jones is a very good employee and manager. We shall never forget that. But we must fill her position. If she should return, well ... we'll cross that bridge when it comes. My partners Bill Smith, Charlie Burt and myself really feel like Martha Seamen would be the perfect person for the position."

Gia's face goes from smiles to shit. *I'll fuck you up. You promised me a better position.*

Ted continues, "Now the person that will fill Martha's position, we choose Janise Thompson."

They all fake clap again.

"Mrs. Thompson's position will be held by Sherry Wong. Mrs. Wong's position goes to Gia Shirley."

"What?! What?!" Gia yells over the loud clapping. All eyes fall on her. "I mean what, I can't believe it. I just started here and I'm an administrative assistant already. Wow, you all really looked out. Making me part of this family. Thanks so much, Sirs." She fakes a smile, taking a seat. Her blood is boiling.

"It was Janise's idea." He hits her with a low blow, thinking about the little gerbil trick.

"There's some cake, punch and donuts. Eat up."

The bosses exit the room. People start whispering and gossiping. Gia exits as well. She's so pissed she doesn't know what hit her. She wants Allen's position so Martha will have to go is all she can think about while entering the restroom. She starts pacing the floor, biting on her bottom lip, hitting the walls. Gia has lost her mind.

Day 12

"How do you like your new desk and office?" Sherry inquires as Gia sets up her new very small office.

"It'll do for now," Gia yawps.

"I don't know about you but I love my new office, this little office ... well, if you call it an office. It was cramping my style. I knew I would move up soon." Gia sizes her up as she continues to talk. "Gia, you can always look at it this way—even though you don't get overtime now and you have this small ass office, at least you do have a job with benefits. I know the Temp agency paid more overtime but $40,000 a year isn't bad for starters," she tells Gia like she cares.

"You know what, Sherry? You're so right. Thank you. I never looked at it that way, Sherry," Gia calls her name as she arranges her flowers, setting them in her small window seal. She pauses and turns, giving Sherry a stare. "I can call you Sherry, right?" Now Gia waits for her permission with her brow raised.

"Sure."

"Can we be friends? You know, start fresh? I'm part of the family now?"

Sherry can't believe her ears. "We sure can. I thought you'd never ask."

"Good. That makes me feel much better. Why don't you stop passed my office tonight around six. We can have some drinks. You know, to celebrate our new accomplishments," Gia invites, holding up a bottle of champagne and two flute glasses.

"Hell yeah, girl. Now you talking. Hell, we can pop the cork now," she tells Gia.

"Girl, I wish. Mr. Smith would have our heads if we drink during business hours," Gia reminds her who they work for.

"I guess you're right. So meet me in my office at six. Much more space," Sherry jokes, observing her old office. "You know we'll have to be quick 'cause I've gotta meet my mother by seven."

"Oh, it will be very quick," Gia lets her know, moving her head up and down as if she knows something Sherry doesn't.

"Alright, see you then!" Sherry exclaims with cheer.

"Yes, I'll see you then," Gia returns.

Day 13

It's six on the nose. Everyone in the office has left for today. Gia grabs the bottle of champagne, heads down the hall to Sherry's office, strutting up to Sherry's desk.

"Hey, girl, I'm almost done. Have a seat," Sherry acknowledges.

Gia takes a seat at the round table that sits in the middle of Sherry's office. No more than two minutes pass. Sherry joins her.

"Thanks for wanting to be my friend. I never had one. You know, since my father died. He was the only friend I had," Sherry tells her.

"He was?"

"Yeah, my boyfriend left me. We were together since 6th grade but he left me for a white lady fifteen years older than him."

"Damn, now that's fucked up," Gia lets on like she really cares.

"Yeah, but the crazy thing is I still love him and I have to see him every day."

"Why every day?" Gia wonders.

"He works here. You may have seen him. Ricky. He's head of the Blackout accounts. He's married to Janise."

"Janise? Old lady Janise? So that's why she don't like being called Mrs. She's tryna stay young. Old hag. But she is nice. So maybe I should be nice." Gia tries to throw her off.

"That bitch ain't nice. She slept with Ted to move her way to the top and she took my man. Now she's sleeping with Ted again. I don't know what she has over'em but whatever it is she's using it. How do you think she got her job? She only has a high school diploma, and for that position you need a master's degree." She gives Gia the 411.

"That's some heavy shit you just laid on me."

"Yeah it is, being as though I have my masters and I've applied for that job three times over."

"It looks like you need to drop down and get yo eagle, girl," Gia teases and starts laughing.

"Never that. Only lowlife hoes do shit like that, feel me?" Janise says, sipping on her bubbly.

"I feel you. But I've gotta get this stuff outta my old desk and meet with Bill—I mean Mr. Smith," Gia corrects herself.

"Bill? Bill left ... he's gone to New York," she informs Gia.

"New York? Why didn't he tell me that?"

"Did you miss the memo? You don't work for him anymore. If you check your email you'll find his memo about going to the New York office. Most of the time he'll leave all the staff a memo on the internet. He left about thirty minutes ago. He's going to that office to see his wife and his old flame." Sherry is trying to let her know about Bill's past.

"I know about his old flame, which was his old assistant. But his wife works in the New York office?"

"Yep. Charlie Burt, that's his ex-wife but we still call her the wife 'cause they act like they're still married," she informs. "She never changed her name to Smith."

"But I just sent flowers to his wife at his home here in DC." Gia is baffled.

"That's his real wife. Get this: she stays home and takes care of his ex mother-in-law while his ex-wife is in New York for six months at a time. Every year for their anniversary Charlie sends the ex-wife flowers, diamonds and furs. It's a strange relationship, I must admit myself. They have some secret past. I don't know what it is but he loves her and she loves him. They will do anything for one another. But whatever happened 20 something years ago he never forgave her. He married Betty. We think 'cause she has money. *Old* money. Charlie's late father is the founder of this company. Now Bill has more shares in this company than her father. For some reason he left the company to Bill and Bill brought Ted on, then later Charlie came into play. Now get this: Charlie's ass is bisexual so who knows what's going on wit' them all." Janise spills all the gossip.

"Girl, now that's a *Lifetime* story within itself," Gia yaps.

"It sho nuff is."

They giggle.

"See you. And thanks for the 411," Gia utters, making her way out the door after downing the rest of her drink.

Sherry isn't that bad at all. Maybe she'll get to keep her life. As far as Mrs. Burt … so she's a woman—and she's gay. I must pay her a visit. Nothing like doing the boss's wife. That shit sounds like fun, Gia thinks to herself as she enters her tiny office.

Day 14

Gia walks in PG hospital.

"Those are beautiful flowers you have," the nurse on the third floor compliments.

"Oh, thank you. They're for a wonderful and dear person to me."

"And who might that be?" the nurse asks Gia.

"Mrs. Jones. Allen Jones."

"Oh, yes. Mrs. Jones. She's in room 340. You know she came out of her coma two days ago."

Gia plays it off because that's news to her ears. "Yes, I know. That's why I'm here to see her."

"Now you must know her breathing is still a little short. We've been taking her on and off the breathing machine so please don't have her talking a lot 'cause she loves to talk," the nurse adds.

"I will keep that in mind ... Mrs. Day," Gia says after reading her badge.

"Oh, where you from?" the nurse asks.

"Mississippi."

"That's the country twang."

"Yes, it comes out now and again." Gia acts it out to the tee.

"We supposed to take your name and ID but I'll let you go. Your hands are full and you seem like a nice young lady."

"That's mighty kind of you, Mrs. Day. I'll just be a few. I know she needs to get much rest."

Gia walks to Allen's room. When she enters, Allen looks up at Gia and tries to say hi. Gia rushes her, pulling her pillow from under her head. Allen is bewildered. She has no idea what is going on. Her eyes widen, she's breathing rapidly. With a firm grip, Gia places the pillow over her mouth. Allen is moving around like a fish out of water as Gia smothers her to death. When she sees Allen stop moving she lifts the pillow, bends over, putting her ear to her mouth to see if she is still breathing.

"Good, that's that. Sorry, I can't have any witness," she whispers, placing the pillow back under her head neatly.

She fixes her clothes, walks out the room, taking the stairway so no one will see her. Gia hurries to her car, gets in, drives off expeditiously.

She pulls into a gas station about 20 minutes down the road, goes in the restroom, pulls out a plastic bag, takes off her wig, glasses, blue contacts, bamboo earrings and she changes her clothes. She places everything in the bag, then she exits the restroom, hops back in her car, drives down the road. She turns into an alley and dumps the evidence in a big construction Dumpster. Then it's off to work. Gia walks in the office looking and smelling good as if nothing happened a few hours ago.

"Hi, Gia, I put a stack of folders on your desk. Mrs. Janise Thompson wants to see you," Mr. Smith's new Administrative Assistant informs her.

"Thanks." She goes to Janise's office. "You wanted to see me?" Gia stands at her desk.

"Yes. The files that are on your desk, please input the info then print it and put it on all the department heads' desks by Monday. So that means the weekend is work for you."

Gia takes her orders but she's not liking it. She hates to work on her off days.

She walks back to her office. Before she enters, she heads back to Bill's office area.

"Cathy, you know what? When I make it to the top I'm taking you with me," she informs his new assistant.

"I would love to work for you, Gia," she says with a smile. "Oh, I almost forgot Mr. Ricky Thompson would like for you to come to his office to pick up the Blackout list."

"Thanks. Can you call him to let him know I'm on my way? Can you inform Sherry in about 30 minutes? Tell her that he would also like to see her. I forgot to tell her last night. I was supposed to have met her in her office at six, but I got busy."

"Will do," Cathy returns.

Gia rides the elevator to the second floor. The elevator doors open.

Fuck, his floor is huge. And who in the hell are all these people? Where they come from? I've neva seen any of 'em before, she thinks to herself as she walks up to the receptionist desk.

"Hi, how may I help you?"

"I'm Gia Shirley from—"

"I know who you are. It's a pleasure to meet you. Mr. Thompson is waiting for you in his office. It's down that hall, make a left then a right, then another left. You can't miss it. It's the huge oval office," she directs.

"Ma'am what goes on, on this floor?" Gia needs to know.

"This is where all the out of state claims are worked on. Twelve states to be exact," the lady informs her.

"Is that right? Who is in charge of these accounts?"

"Charlie Burt. This is their department. She comes to town every six months. She's a doll."

"Yes, I heard. Well thanks for the info. I guess I'll make my way to his office."

"Anytime, Mrs. Shirley."

J.J. Jackson

***

Gia strolls in Ricky's office. "You called? You wanted to see me?"

Ricky's not a bad looking brother, with his dark skin six five, wavy hair, full goatee, low cut sideburns and a full beard neatly groomed. He turns around, sitting in his office chair.

"Don't I always?" he answers with a sexy voice.

Gia smiles as she moves up to her old sex partner, leaning across the front of his desk. He knew her five years earlier. They met in New Jersey.

"So I finally met wifey and the ex. That would be baby momma. She was filling me in on some of your little secrets. I see you haven't changed one bit," Gia tells him.

"Now, now, little Gia. Let's not waste time talking," he tells her, pulling out his manhood.

"*Mmm,* my little friend. Shit, he still looks good enough to eat." She licks her lips.

"Huh, your friend misses those lips too," he returns.

Gia slowly walks around the desk. She turns Ricky's oversized office chair around, gets on her knees, taking hold of his soft dick, placing it in between her lips. His dicks grows in seconds from the wetness, the sizzling heat of her tongue. She's enjoying all nine inches of his pretty dick. As she gives him long slow strokes, she looks into his eyes.

"You like?" she says with half her mouth full.

"Indeed. Indeed I do," he informs, moving his head up and down.

Gia gets off her knees, turns, unties her brown wrap dress, allowing it to fall to the floor exposing her two perfect round shaped ass cheeks.

"Yes, *oh yes,*" he moans, resting his head on the chair, straightening his legs out.

Gia straddles him backwards. She lowers her pussyhole to the head of his huge black dick. She lowers and lowers, then she butterflies his dick back and forth to the tip and back down over and over, real slow. He meets her every stroke as he pumps, slowing to her rhythm.

"*Ummm* yes, Rick. Yes, baby *pleazz* don't stop," she begs as she continues to wind on his dick.

"Turn around, Gia," he demands of her in a low soft voice. Ricks lifts her up in the air with his masculine arms, sticking his dick back in her dripping hot wet ripe pussy. He strokes and strokes every morsel of her tenderness.

"Oh shit fuck me that's it right there don't stop *please.* Oh Rick, damn I needed this!" she's yelling now, not giving a damn who hears her.

He stuffs her underwear in her mouth to shut her up. Rick's banging and pushing, pumping and thrusting his king-size dick up in her.

"Gia. Hell, Gia, you the only bitch that can take this dick on. Oh shit, Gia." He slides his dick out and slides it in her asshole. The feeling he's delivering is astonishing. She can't hold back anymore.

"Rick, here it comes! Here it comes!"

"Nut, baby, nut!" he tells her. He looks up towards the door. "What the fuck?!" he utters, but he doesn't stop. His eyes are fixated on the person that's staring at him but he can't stop, he's gotta get his nut first. Gia is in another world. She continues to enjoy the dick he's putting on her.

"Rick, *my ass my ass,* I'm cumming!" she yells out.

"Awww shit, Gia, baby. Me too, me too!" he whispers, pulling his dick out after about 3 more strokes. He lowers Gia onto the floor.

Sherry is stuck. She doesn't know what to say. As Gia puts her thug on and fixes her dress, she notices Rick is staring at the door while he's pulling his pants up. He's not saying a word. She follows his eyes.

"Sherry, nice of you to join us. How long you been standing there?" Gia knows full well she told Cathy to tell her to meet Rick in 30 minutes.

When she musters up some spit, "You BITCH!" Sherry says through clinched teeth while standing in the doorway of Rick's office holding onto the knob.

"You ain't neva lied about that," Gia says. She's laughing.

Sherry looks at Rick and shakes her head. "The more things change the more they stay the same. Rick, what if it was your wife that walked in the door on you? Oh, I almost forgot—would you care? Hell, Ted's boning her anyway," Sherry spits venom then she exits his office, slamming the door.

Rick looks at Gia. "She never comes down here during the day. Never."

Gia gives him a shy look, hunching her shoulders.

"Oh no you didn't," he tells her.

"Oh but I did."

"Gia, not cool. Not cool at all."

"It's nothing I can't handle. You know how I do it."

"No, Gia, this ain't New Jersey and I don't know how you do it."

"Forget about her. I have something I need you to help me with."

"What might that be?" he asks, irritated now.

"I want you to help me make it to the top."

"What does that mean, make it to the top? I'ing in no position to promote you."

She grabs his cheeks and squeezes them together. "I know you not. But you can talk to Charlie. I know she'll listen to you."

"What position do you want?"

"Your wife's."

"My wife's? Gia, now you done lost it for real."

"No, you're going to lose it if you don't play your part in this."

"What you mean? I'm gon' lose what?" He's getting more irritated.

"You know what, don't worry about it. I'll just take your job. How about that?"

"Gia, you're buggin'," he tells her.

She sees he's feeling uneasy about what she just said so she seduces him all over again. He falls for the bait, and when he cums three times over:

"Gia, I'ma see what I can do," he tells her, wiping his dick off with baby wipes.

Gia heads out the door.

The power of the P-U-S-S-Y. She wears a smile on her face as she walks up the hall.

Day 15

Gia walks in Sherry's office. "Hi, you. I came to bring peace. I'm sorry about yesterday. That just happened."

"Gia, please leave my office. If you want to speak with me, please make an appointment."

Gia inspects her face, thinking she's got to be kidding. "Are you that mad about a piece of dick? Girl, I used to know him. We been fuckin' for years. He's a man hoe. Why would you want to be with someone like that anyway? Sherry, you're selling yourself short."

"I'm not selling myself any kind of way. To me, you're the man hoe and he's a jerk off. I don't care what you two do, as long as he takes care of our child. I'm a grown woman. I can take care of myself. Gia, I don't befriend people then shit on'em like you just did."

"Ok, I get it. I'm sorry. I see we come from two different worlds, this is clear. I see that now. So I'll leave you be. However, I want you to know I mean what I said. You deserve more than tricky Ricky."

Gia makes her last remarks as she leaves the office.

"These sensitive bitches. They need to come to my class of the hard knock life."

Gia goes to Ted's office, walking in without asking. "You son of a bitch! You did me wrong you knew I wanted more than admin of the fucking upper offices!"

"Gia, I couldn't just make you operations manager. What you think this is?" he spits. "And lower your voice. Someone may hear you."

Like Gia cares. Putting both hands on the front of his desk, she leans towards him. "You do know I recorded our session that day when I cuffed you."

His eyes grow huge. "Gia, are you blackmailing me?"

"What do you think? You know what, ask Janise sense you boning her too."

"Who told you that lie? Janise and I have never—"

She cuts him off, reaching across his desk giving him a soft smack on his face. "I know you put that little thing you call a dick in'a. That's why you moved her up over me. She only has a high school diploma. I have my masters. Now you fix this, or that tape goes viral."

"Viral? As in the internet viral?"

"You got it. Now you get me operations. I worked hard for it. I don't fuck with white men … well for the money I do. But that's here nor there. Just get me the damn position," she notes as she vanishes, leaving him sitting behind his desk worried about the repercussions if that tape leaks.

21 DAYS OF SECRETS

***

Bill calls Gia into his office.

"Yes you called me, Bill?"

"Yes, I did. Take a seat, please."

"Are you going to introduce me to the lady?" Gia asks, watching the older lady that's standing by his chair.

"This is Charlie Burt's mother."

"Hi, Gia. My name is Mrs. Burt. You can call me Seria."

"Hi, Seria. Nice to meet you," Gia says, taking a seat in front of his desk.

"Gia, I guess you're wondering what I brought you in here for?"

"Kinda," she voices, not taking her eyes off Seria.

"I brought you in to talk about the Error in the Hold accounts. Ted and I spoke about this. We came up with creating a new department, calling it Error in the Hold accounts. This department will consist of 20 employees and one operations manager. It will have a million-dollar budget for payroll the first year. The operational manager will be offered a salary of $200,000 the first year, receiving a commission bonus at the end of each year. The office will be on the 4th floor of this building. I have computers up there. We were going to do this a while ago but it kinda got put on the back burner. So I am offering this project to you. Ted informed me you did such a good job when you were helping him out. He added you have an eye for errors. Is this something you would like to do?" he asks.

Gia can't contain her excitement. "Yes, yes. I'll take it all, thanks." She smiles ear to ear.

"Good. For the time being, we're pulling you from your duty as admin. You'll move upstairs and start going through files manually. I'll send you five people to help you until we can get the computer programmers up there. The phones are on already. You'll interview the staff that may apply for the position. Let me know what date you would like for us to list the positions."

"Thanks so much. I won't let you down."

"No, don't let Ted down. He's the one that convinced me to do this. And Gia, please no more blackmails. It's not a good look for you."

Gia's smile quickly dissolves. She can't believe he said that in front of Mrs. Burt.

"You're dismissed," he tells her coldly.

Mrs. Burt follows her out the office. "Gia, Gia," she calls in a low voice.

Gia makes an about face.

"Can we meet for lunch?" she asks her.

"Sure. You wanna meet me after you heard that?"

"Chile, who cares about that? We women do what it takes. What woman you know that's on top hasn't slept their way there? My husband owned this piece of shit and many a women slept with him to make it to the top. So I'll meet you at Tony and Joes at 8 p.m. tomorrow, if you know where that is."

"Sounds good to me," Gia lets out.

"Good." Mrs. Burt's smile sticks to her face as she walks away.

Day 16

"I wonder what she wants to see me about," Gia says as she sits at her kitchen table eating bacon, eggs and drinking her morning coffee.

Three hours later Gia walks in the office. People are gathered around.

"Gia, did you hear what happened?" Cathy asks.

"No, what happened?" she asks Cathy, Bill's clerk.

"It's Sherry. She got into a car accident. Her brakes went out. She hit a truck head on."

"OMG!" Gia lets out, holding her mouth. "Tell me she's alright?"

"Yes, thank God. But her child is dead. Her and Mr. Thompson's child is dead."

"Her what? My God, where is she?" Gia says.

"At home. She's taking the week off. He is too."

"Shouldn't she take more than that? I mean both of them?"

"Yeah, but she said she wants to get back to work soon. It's for the best, she said. He has too much work to do, he told Bill." Cathy relies the gossip.

"I'll send her flowers. What's her address?" Gia asks with a nice cheese on her face.

"Hold on, let me look." Cathy looks in her computer. She prints it out then hands it to Gia. "Would you rather I do it for you, Gia?"

"No, I'll take care of it."

Gia leaves the second floor, taking the stairway.

"I killed her child. Forgive me, Lord. I didn't mean for her child to die. I bled the brakes thinking she would be in the car alone. But she wasn't, that's my fault. I'm sorry, Lord, I am. I would never kill a child. I will make it up to her, I promise," she continues to express, crying real tears.

She feels so guilty. For once in her life she feels pain in her heart for someone else.

Not being able to get nothing done today, she turns out the lights to her new plush office, making her way to meet Mrs. Burt.

"Goodnight you all, thanks for working overtime. I greatly appreciate it," she tells the four staff members that stayed so they can make overtime monies.

She gets in her car, drives to Georgetown parks, makes her way into Tony and Joe's restaurant.

"Hello, I'm looking for a Mrs. Burt," she tells the hostess at the front door.

The hostess reads over her roster. "I found her. Follow me," she orders.

Gia follows her.

"Here you are, the VIP room. Would you like something to drink while you wait for your waiter?" she offers.

"Yes, a tall glass of red wine. Any kind," Gia tells her, kinda wondering why it's another lady with Mrs. Burt.

"Hi, Gia," Seria greets happily.

"Hi." Gia smiles

Charlie rises out her chair in slow motion. Tears fill her eyes. "It is you. Gia, my Gia."

"What, lady? Who are you?" Gia raises concern.

Seria stands beside Gia. "Gia, this is your mother. My daughter, Charlie."

Gia stares at the both of them back and forth. "My what?"

"Gia, will you please give us a minute of your time so I can explain this all to you. I know this sounds crazy but I think after you hear us out you will understand," Charlie speaks up.

Gia hesitates, thinking she is one of the company head bosses so she sits.

Charlie sits across from her so she can get a good look at her long lost child.

"Gia?" Seria calls. "I have some pictures here." She pulls them out her TOD's purse. "Gia, this is your two sisters, Sandy and Xian. I raised Xian until she was 16 years old. She fell ill of a rare blood disease. She died. I make it a point to visit her grave every day, making sure she has fresh flowers. Charlie comes down every six months. We celebrate her birthday every year together. Sandy ... we don't know who adopted her. We thought you two were being raised together. We found out that wasn't so, that Sandy moved to another home. Her parents said they couldn't handle her anymore. We searched and searched for the both of you, coming up with nothing. Both adoptions were what they call *closed* adoptions.

"When you all were born, Charlie was 14. My husband, her father, threatened to disown her from the family, meaning she would've been put out with nowhere to go and no money. So I sent her to my sister's house and told him she gave you all up but I kept one of you. He said that was ok after he got used to her. My friend took you two so we could see you all, but when her husband left her she sold you two without telling me. Old bitch, I hate her to this day for it. Well the lady she sold you to put you two up for adoption when she went broke. That is how we lost the two of you. Believe me when I say I wish things could have been different."

Gia is so shocked but happy her parents are happy to see her. Now she understands why Bill was standoffish. *Makes sense now.*

Gia lifts out her seat, runs around the table hugging her mother for the first time. She's so happy to meet her. She knows now she'll be loved by the woman she thought didn't love or want her. It feels good to know she was wanted.

Day 17

Gia called her sister Sandy. She didn't want her mother and grandmother to know she talked to her 'cause she wasn't sure if Sandy wanted to be in their life. She tells Sandy everything they told her. Sandy said she didn't want to meet them. She didn't ever want them to know she was alive. She told Gia she just wanted to keep playing the twin game at the company. No one notices when she is Sandy or Gia. She likes that. She hates Charlie even more now for not picking her over the other twin to take care of. For letting them go over money. This she lets Gia know.

Gia was sad for her but she told her she respects that. She'll do anything for her sister. She feels she has to. She was born one hour older than Sandy, plus Sandy had it hard with her adopted family being beaten all the time. At least that's what she told Gia.

Sandy sits on the sofa in Gia's living room watching TV.

"Gia, why you still living in here we making all this money?"

"I'on know. I think I'm attached to it. I've been in here for so long. Plus I like apartment living. All that big house stuff is you. Not me," she explains.

"Oh well. I think we need a new place," Sandy says.

"Whatever you say. Why don't you go and get a new place? We spilt the money 50-50 anyways."

"You right. I'll think about it. My apartment is falling apart anyway. But this is what I came to tell you. I got this gig. Merry said he thinks we can make at least two million off it each."

"Oh yeah? What kind of gig is it?" Gia asks while cooking dinner for them.

"We gon' rob this bank. He know the lady that runs it. She gon' turn off the cameras while we rob the joint. She told him four million would be in the vault. We'll just go in, get the money, split it three ways. Sounds easy, right?"

"Yap. When he gonna do it?" Gia questions.

"Tomorrow at 6 a.m. when the bank lady is opening up," she informs.

"Let's do it. But this is the last scam for me. I just wanna get to know my family and be loved. I wanna be square."

"Fine then," Sandy says, frowning up her face at Gia.

Gia brings the food to the table. "I may have to leave you here. I gotta meet Mrs. Burt. We're going to the movies."

"Gia, we always eat dinner together since we been back together. What's going on with you? This family shit is getting to your head."

"No it's not. I just wanna get to know them like I get to know you. What's wrong with that? They're not taking me from you at all. It's not like that," Gia tries to explain.

"Gia, when you start liking the movies? We always watch them in the house."

"I know but tonight I'm watching a movie with my grandmother. Now eat up."

Sandy looks at her food. "I'm not hungry," she pouts, walking out the front door.

Day 18

It's 5:30 a.m. Gia, Merry, and Sandy sit outside the SunTrust Bank. The lady drives up. They all approach her wearing black masks. She acts shocked. Hurrying, she opens the door to the bank taking them to the vault. They hurry, collecting all the money they can fit into the gray bags.

"Ok, I'll pick mines up at your house, Mary," the lady that runs the back says.

"No you won't."

Bloc! Bloc!

Two shots ring out.

"Why you kill'em both?"

"'Cause two is bedda than four. Now let's go before people start coming in."

They ride back to the apartment.

"What we gon' do wit' all this money?" one of them speaks out.

"Spend it, what else? Four million—two for you, two for me," one of them says.

They laugh. They start running around the apartment, throwing money in the air.

"We're rich for real!" they yell.

"Ok look, I'ma see you tomorrow. Don't be spending all this money around here. Keep your job for a while, then after shit dies down you can start spending. Buy nice stuff, you get it?"

"I do, don't worry."

"I can't believe you shot her."

Day 19

"Hello, Gia," Sherry says as she enters Gia's office.

"Hello," she speaks back. "Sorry about your child again," Gia sincerely tells her for the fifth time.

"I know you are. Just checking on you. Sorry about that day I got upset with you. I know I told you but I'm sorry."

"It's ok. Look, Sherry, I have so much to do. Can we talk lata?"

"Oh, ok. Are you going to hire me up here with you?" Sherry asks.

Gia looks at her. "No, I got enough people working here already."

"Oh. Oh, but I thought that night you came to see me and we ... you know, had fun. You and me ..." Sherry is confused.

Looking at Sherry, "That was to make you feel bedda. Sherry, you too weak to be my woman. Now I told you I got shit to do," she says, putting her head down, reading her papers.

Sherry eyes start to water. She leaves Gia's office in a rage. She stops at Bill's office.

"Mr. Smith, you have one minute."

He sees it's her. "Sure, come in."

"Thanks. It's about Gia. I think she killed all your employees. I think she tried to kill me that day, not knowing my child would be in the car."

Bill tells her to keep it to herself. He tells her to let him take care of it, thanking her again. Before she exits his office, "Did you tell anyone else this story?"

"No, but I didn't want you to be next, you know. So I thought I would tell you first."

"Thanks again. I'll handle it. And be looking for something extra on your paycheck for being brave enough to come by and tell me."

"You welcome," she tells him, walking out his office snickering.

He calls his ex-wife to his office, telling her what Sherry told him.

"We'll handle it. Call her to the office," Charlie demands.

He calls Gia to his office.

She walks in. "You call me?"

"Yes baby girl we did." He tells her what Sherry told them.

"You want me to handle it, dad?" she asks. He's not used to being called dad but he likes it.

Charlie looks at him, waiting for an answer. "What?! That would be a murder and we would be in on it," he tells her.

"Bill, I just got her back. I'm not losing her to prison. No, not happening. So either you have her killed or you let her do what she's been doing to make it to the top."

"How did you know it was me?" Gia asks.

"I put two and two together when you blackmailed Ted," Bill assures her. He's not stupid.

"Oh."

"Ok, just do what you do and be careful—in which I'm sure you will."

Day 20

"Gia, here are the names for the party." Bill's new assistant hands them to her.

"OK. I'll take care of them," she says, walking to her office.

"Hi, Gia," Janise Says with glee walking past her in the hall.

"Hi, Janise," she speaks back. She's wondering why she's speaking to her. Only if she knew she had her man for dinner last night.

She makes it to her office.

"Good morning, Mrs. Shirley. The designer of the new mansion you're buying called. He said call him. He needs to go over some things about the plans with you. Mr. Tattaes called as well about your new Lexus coupe. He said to call him immediately, something about the insurance number. He left off the last digit. And do you want me to send Ms. Sherry Wong's family some flowers?" Cathy, Bill's old assistant, asks.

Gia kept her promise and took her with her. She's paying her more money. She stops in her tracks. "Mrs. Wong? What happened to her?" Gia asks.

"She died in the garage around 4 o'clock yesterday after work."

"Wait. What did they say happened to her?"

"The police don't know. All they saying is she dropped dead. They won't know until the autopsy."

"Man, that's crazy."

"That's what I said."

"Send them some flowers, by all means," she orders Cathy.

She walks in her office, closes the door laughing. "Got yo ass. So that's why Janise so happy today. That's why she spoke to me. She thinks her competition is dead. Little do she know. Life's not bad here. I could quit this job but it feels good to be at the top, looking down on muthafuckas for a change. I think I'll stay right here. And see what's in store for me. Maybe I'll become the owner one day. Soon ... really soon."

Day 21

She leaves her job after a hard day's work. She drives to the Catholic church not too far from where her office is. Parking, she gets out. Walking in Gia stands in line to see the priest to give her confession. She's the last person for today. Taking her seat in the booth, she starts confessing her sins.

"Forgive me, Father, for I have sinned."

"What have you done, my child?"

"For the last 21 days I've been killing people. I injected poison into a stranger's neck. She's dead. I poisoned a lady on my job, then I smothered her. She died too. I was partly the reason for a child's death that I will regret for the rest of my life. I also gave her mother some killer mushrooms in her pepper steak. She died. Then I killed a bank teller. Oh, I lied on my application to get my job. I said I went to Harvard so they would hire me for this job. I also blackmailed a man."

The priest is silent, also shocked. He doesn't know what to do. *I can't call the police and report this*, are his thoughts as he sits on the other side of the makeshift confession booth. The real one is under construction so they had to make a temporary one.

"Is there anything else?" he asks.

She quickly walks out her side of the booth into his. Raising the long knife, "It's one more thing. I killed my sista at a bank robbery! I'm Sandy!"

The following is an excerpt from Michell'a & Akasha's:

When The Dimes Drop

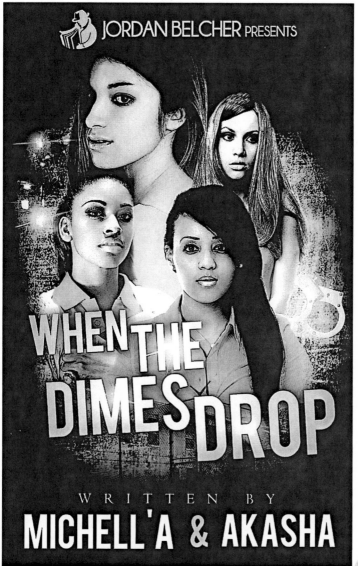

JORDAN BELCHER PRESENTS

WHEN THE DIMES DROP

WRITTEN BY
MICHELL'A & AKASHA

PROLOGUE

"ORDER! ORDER! ORDER!" the federal judge yelled over the buzz and noise from media, friends and family of both—defendants and victims.

The large courtroom was packed. After 4 days of deliberation the 12-person jury had finally returned with a verdict.

"Will the defendants please rise?" the judge said as the jury sat down. "Does the jury have a verdict?" he continued.

The three disheveled women all stood. Ongell Addis, Cheyenne Redwood and Monet Murray rose and faced the jury. It had all come down to this.

Their dream team of attorneys attempted to look hopeful and confident, but they all knew. Out of the 118 counts being held against their clients it was pretty much destined that they would be found guilty on some counts. Especially when 21 of the counts were murders.

The three women had already assumed the same.

"Will the jury please read the verdict?" the judge ordered. Outside of cameras snapping, the courtroom was completely silent.

"On count one: we the jury find the defendants, not guilty." The women all held hands and smiled. Only 117 more not guilties. "On count two: we the jury find the defendants, not guilty." "On count three: we the jury find the defendants, not guilty."

"Hold on jurors," the judge said. "Hey, I demand absolute silence inside of this courtroom. Anything outside of silence and I will clear everyone except jurors, prosecutors, defendants, counselors and myself out! Is that understood?" the judge ordered the courtroom as the reporters and onlookers grew noisy after the 3 not guilties.

Everyone got quiet.

"Ok. Jury, continue please."

"On count four: we the jury find the defendants, not guilty."

"On count five: we the jury find the defendants, *guilty.*"

"On count six: we the jury find the defendants, *guilty.*"

"On count seven: we the jury find the defendants *guilty.*"

"On count eight: we the jury find the defendants ..."

The jury foreman would go on for close to an hour reading off one-hundred and fourteen counts, 114 guilties. Including 21 homicides, multiple counts of extortion, drug trafficking, assaults, 30 conspiracies to commit murder, racketeering, 1 Continuing Criminal Enterprise and a slew of other federal felonies.

"Jury, is that your final verdict?" the judge asked the foreman. "Yes, Your Honor, it is."

"Well ok, due to the magnitude of this indictment I will not be issuing a sentence today. This court will be in recess until January 18th. That's giving this court 90 days to fully review this case and determine a proper judgement and sentence. Thank you jury for your help. It's been a long drawn out proceeding and I appreciate you all's patience."

"Before I put this court in recess, counselors I'll hear any type of pre-sentence and/or appellate motions in my chambers. Due to the media frenzy surrounding this case, I'm really in a rush to clear out this courtroom. You agree?"

All the attorneys (prosecutors and defense counsel) nodded that they understood.

"Ok then. This court is in recess. Thank you," the judge said and banged his gavel.

Court was adjourned. The media agglomerated as it exited the courtroom, all trying to get the story out on the verdict.

"Damn dawg. A hunnit and fo'teen guilties," Ongell Addis moaned.

"That bitch told on us, bro," Cheyenne Redwood stated.

"We through," Ongell said again, moreso to herself.

"We are going to file an immediate appeal, citing circumstantial evidence. The testimony of a jailhouse rat shouldn't be the sole cause of 114 guilty verdicts," one of the 6 lawyers said as all 9 people sat in a conference/waiting room.

"Yeah, do that," Monet Murray told him.

"This is fucked up, we got mo' counts than John Gotti," Ongell said.

"Maan, fuck all that ... I rode 13 years out wit' that bitch! I did 13 years wit' that bitch, not including the shit when she got locked back up. I had her right when she got out. And this bitch told on us!" Cheyenne yelled out.

"I'ma kill that bitch," Monet said.

"How?" Ongell asked. "Wit' 114 guilty verdicts. That bitch on the bricks, free like O.J. We through. Twenty-one M's? Twenty-one, bro! We gon' die in the Feds. I just got through doin' 300 months. It's over. We won't be able to ice that bitch. I seen hoes grow old and die in the Feds. Now I'm about to be one of them," Ongell cried without tears.

"Only way I'ma die in the Feds is gettin' shot while hoppin' a muthafuckin' fence," Cheyenne stated matter-of-factly.

"Straight up," Monet agreed.

"Hold on, ladies. There's still legal maneuverings we can take," said a high-priced lawyer.

"Niggas don't win appeals in the Feds," Ongell spoke.

"They do," an attorney stated with confidence. "And we will."

"Let's not lose focus here, ladies," yet another attorney told the trio.

"Lose focus ... lose focus? Nigga, is you serious! We just lost in trial one hundred and fourteen times, mutha-fucka!" Ongell yelled.

The attorney turned red and pointed his finger in her face. "Listen here, lil bitch. I'm not about to let some ex-whore jailhouse mouse beat me. I'll be damned if I lose to some worthless prostitute, snake, jellyfish ass WHORE!" he shouted and spat into Ongell's face.

"Ooooh," Monet jokingly instigated.

"Checkmate," Cheyenne said.

"Queen takes rook. Checkmate!" Monet said and both women began to laugh.

"Damn ok, Meyer," Ongell said in a faked submission. "I'm chillin', ok?"

"Well chill out then," he said, smiling and regaining his composure.

"Can I suck yo dick?" Ongell asked. The entire room erupted in loud, stress-relieving laughter.

Michell'a & Akasha

Back inside their single person cells all 3 women fell into deep thoughts ...

Ongell looked through her legal work and tried to figure out an out. *Is there a possible loop hole? Is there a case law similar to theirs?*

"Damn," she said out loud while looking into a polished steel mirror. "A hundred and fourteen counts. Twenty one bodies. *Gotdamn.*"

She was only on the streets for 7 months after doing the majority of a 25-year federal sentence. Now she faced a potential death sentence.

Monet's mind fell on thoughts of her entire life. She went from an upper-middle class family to Kansas University grad to marijuana queenpin, then she became a porn superstar. She thought about Alicia Eugardo, her ex-lover, now deceased. She had no kids.

"Damn ... It was a helluva ride," she said to herself with a tearful smile as she looked into her scratched up mirror. "Please God, don't let me die in a jail cell or prison infirmary." It wasn't a prayer, per se.

Cheyenne thought about her daughter. She was also in their indictment but hadn't been caught yet. They managed to remain in contact via Cheyenne's lawyers. She hoped that Regina would choose death over prison.

WHEN THE DIMES DROP

"Damn. Damn. My whole life been a bitch," she said to herself, looking at her beautiful disheveled face in the distorted mirror.

She then pulled out a picture of her daughter with her boyfriend Jesus Gusman. *"Damn."*

Text **JORDAN** to **77948**

And stay updated on all of Jordan Belcher Presents' *newest releases, free giveaways,* and *special promotions!*

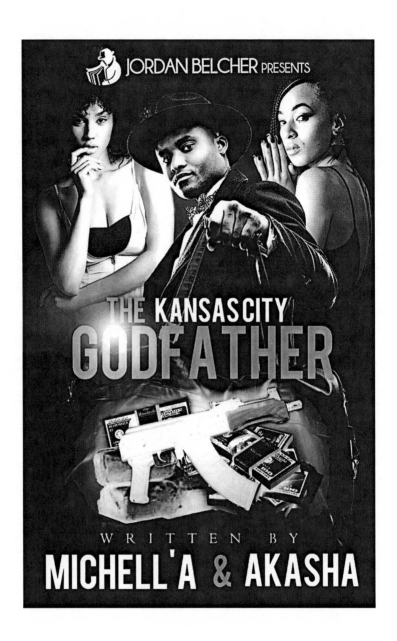

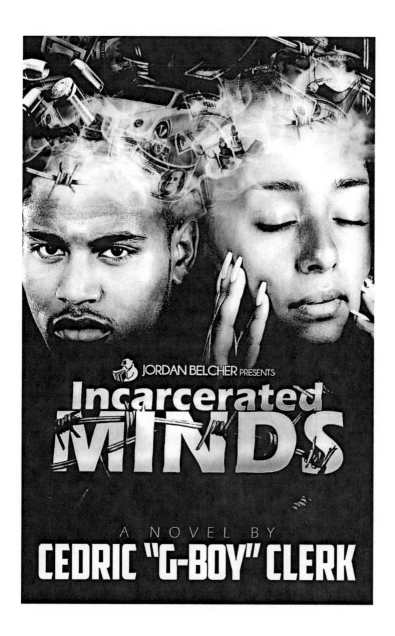

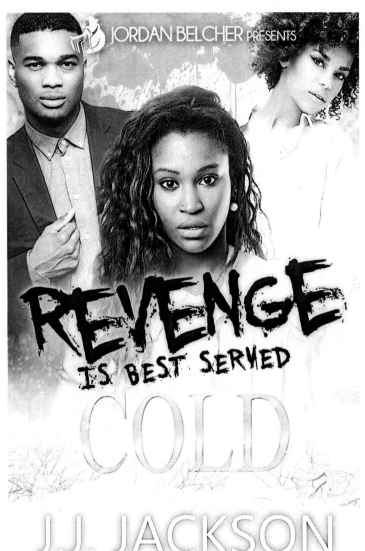

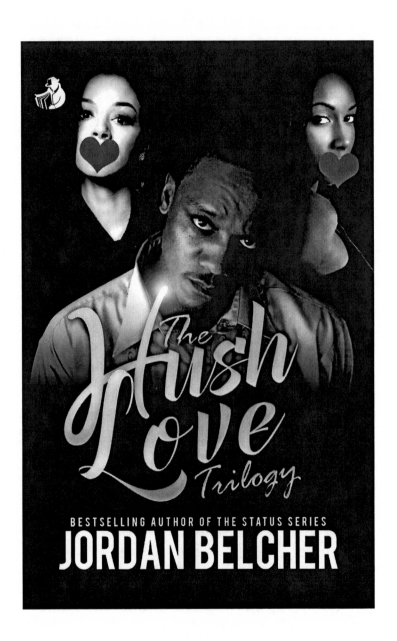

CPSIA information can be obtained
at www.ICGtesting.com
Printed in the USA
LVOW08s2057310817
547127LV00001B/33/P